# Shark Attack

## Judi Peers

James Lorimer & Company Ltd., Publishers
Toronto, 1998

James Lorimer & Company Ltd. acknowledges the support of the Department of Canadian Heritage and the Ontario Arts Council in the development of writing and publishing in Canada. We acknowledge the support of the Canada Council for the Arts for our publishing program.

Cover illustration: Sharif Tarabay

**Canadian Cataloguing in Publication Data**

Peers, Judi, 1956–
    Shark attack
(Sports stories)

ISBN 1-55028-621-8 (bound) ISBN 1-55028-620-X (pbk.)

I. Title. II. Series: Sports series (Toronto, Ont.).
PS8581.E3928S52 1998    jC813'.54    C98-930349-7
PZ7.P33Sh 1998

James Lorimer & Company Ltd.,
Publishers
35 Britain Street
Toronto, Ontario
M5A 1R7

Distributed in the United States
by: Orca Book Publishers,
P.O. Box 468
Custer, WA  USA
98240-0468

Printed and bound in Canada

*For my parents,*
*Lloyd and Dorothy West,*
*who not only taught me*
*to always play to win,*
*but also the fact that*
*you often win simply by*
*playing the game,*
*and for*
*my husband*
*Dave,*
*the most "winning"*
*coach in the country.*

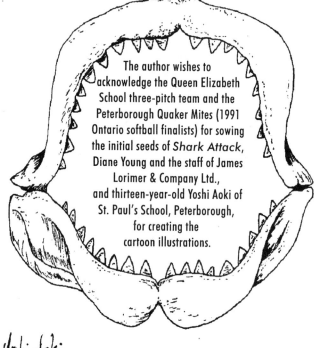

The author wishes to
acknowledge the Queen Elizabeth
School three-pitch team and the
Peterborough Quaker Mites (1991
Ontario softball finalists) for sowing
the initial seeds of *Shark Attack*,
Diane Young and the staff of James
Lorimer & Company Ltd.,
and thirteen-year-old Yoshi Aoki of
St. Paul's School, Peterborough,
for creating the
cartoon illustrations.

# Contents

# 1

## The Sharks

I don't believe it!" Matt Tucker slammed the shiny blue bat into the dirt. Squeezing onto the edge of the bench, he buried his face in his hands.

"No problem," Coach Leahy shouted. "You'll hit it next time."

"Yeah right," Matt muttered. Had Coach totally lost his mind? He had struck out for the third time that game. It was the top of the seventh, their last turn at bat, and none of the East City Sharks had gotten a hit. Two measly foul balls — that was it.

Hesitantly, Ben Aoki, the Sharks' catcher, walked to the plate.

"Back of the box, Ben," Coach yelled, clapping his hands encouragingly. "Get set in there! You can do it!"

"No batter! No batter!" the Lions' bench chanted.

In the back of the batter's box, heart thumping wildly, Ben Aoki shifted his weight from one leg to the other, trying to find a comfortable stance.

Spike McGarrity, the Lakefield Lions' new pitching sensation, rocked cockily on the rubber, then launched his right arm into a fluid windmill motion as he exploded off the mound. His arms were strong and muscular, his form perfect. The ball was in the catcher's mitt by the time Ben had swung.

"Stee-rike one!" boomed the umpire.

Spike pushed the loose tendrils of curly brown hair back into his cap and replanted on the rubber.

The Lions' bench erupted.

> Everywhere we go ... o,
> People want to know ... o,
> Who we are ... r,
> So we tell them.
> We're the Lions,
> Mighty, mighty Lions!

"Mighty big mouths," Matt said, to no one in particular.

Normally the Lions wouldn't stand a chance against the Sharks. Just because they'd signed a new ace chucker, suddenly they were all hot shots.

"Stee-rike two!" The pitch had zoomed in knee-high, catching the outside corner of the plate.

Matt glanced over at Coach Leahy. He was standing in the coach's box wearing red, white, and black, the distinctive colours of the East City Sharks. He was busy talking to the Lions' lanky third baseman. Maybe, just maybe, Matt could get away with it, if he timed it just right and didn't yell too loudly. The guys would all get a laugh and it would sure make him feel a whole lot better.

Matt cupped his hands to his mouth.

> Everybody know ...o's
> Lions pick their no ...

"Matt!" Coach cut him off. "You know the rules. Keep it positive or keep it quiet."

The Sharks' bench fell silent. Coach signalled to Ben at the plate. He adjusted his glasses, touched his cap, nose, and right ear, then drew an *X* across his chest.

Usually, a tap of the cap meant bunt, but the *X* cancelled everything preceding it. Coach was telling Ben to hit away.

Why was the Coach bothering to go through the motions? Matt wondered. They were losing five to nothing. Ben wasn't going to hit this kid.

"Team huddle! Right field!" Coach's voice shattered Matt's thoughts. "Right after the game." A medium-sized man with greying black hair, he spoke with authority. "Clear the bench area quickly, and hustle on out there."

"Stee-rike three!" The man hunched behind home plate yanked off his mask. "Looks like that's the game, folks."

"Looks like that's the season," Ben mumbled a few minutes later as he and Matt trotted toward the small group of players gathered in shallow right field.

Matt didn't hear his teammate. He anxiously twisted his cap in his hands. Coach was a pretty cool guy most of the time, but he was strict too. Was he going to chew him out for yelling at the Lions?

"This Spike McGarrity's the best pitcher I've ever seen," Coach Leahy was saying as Matt and Ben joined the circle. "Heard he moved up here a couple of weeks ago. From California, I think it was. But this is only the first time we've faced him. We'll get onto him." He turned and smiled at Mike Freeburn and Chris Kenton, the pitching duo for the Sharks. "We've got a couple of good pitchers ourselves. You guys put in a little extra work ... who knows? And Matt," he added, a note of sternness creeping into his voice.

Matt's stomach tightened. He looked nervously at the ground and braced himself for a verbal onslaught.

Coach rumpled the centre fielder's sand-coloured hair. "You're one of the team's captains. You're supposed to set a good example. No more nonsense. Okay?"

Matt nodded politely, surprised and relieved that Coach had let him off so easily.

The Sharks hung around for a long time after Coach Leahy had left the ball park, disappointment etched on every face. Why did Spike McGarrity have to move up here? Matt wondered. Of all the places in the entire world, Spike's family just had to go and pick the Peterborough area.

Kate Crowley, the team's left fielder, sighed heavily. "My dad said we had the County Championship in the bag." Tall, skinny, her long auburn hair tucked up under her cap, she was proud to be the only girl to have made the Sharks, one of the teams that was expected to go all the way this year.

"Looks like that bag of yours just sprung one major-league leak," Ben laughed. There was an edge of sarcasm in his voice.

"What are we going to do?" Kate asked, glancing grimly around the circle at the others.

"We've got to do something!" Matt's steel blue eyes narrowed in determination. "We've just got to win that Championship!"

# 2

# The Tuckers

Matt let the heavy wooden door bang loudly behind him as he entered the grey house on Pinehill Drive. A neatly manicured lawn and beautiful garden framed the board-and-batten structure; an intricate white veranda and matching shutters added charming detail to the front of the house. At least that's what the real estate agent had said when she had first showed it to the Tuckers, just six years before. It still looked the same. Like new.

Pinehill Drive was only a few kilometres from East City Bowl, where the Sharks played their home games and held most of their practices. East City was on the east side of the Otonabee River, the river that split the city of Peterborough into two unequal pieces, approximately three-quarters on the west, one-quarter on the east. Most of the merchants in East City had agreed to sponsor one player on Matt's team. He wore "Bryant's Shell," on the back of his uniform. Ben was sponsored by the East City Coffee Shop.

Matt often walked to the park with Ben or rode his bike with a group of the guys. Today, Ben had gone shopping with his mother after the game; Matt had poked his way home, alone.

He tossed his glove and cleats onto the mound of sports equipment in the corner of the mudroom, sending a couple of clean-shaven tennis balls scooting across the floor. "Anybody home?" he called.

"Down here." His father's deep voice floated up faintly from the basement.

Matt descended the stairs into the newly finished family room below. The pungent smell of fresh paint and new carpet still lingered in the air.

Mr. Tucker was tilted back in his favourite easy chair, his dark head and strong body almost hidden by the local newspaper, *The Peterborough Examiner*. "Win your game?" he asked.

Matt shook his head, then muttered a mournful "No," when he realized that his father wasn't looking at him.

"Any hits?"

"No."

Mr. Tucker lifted his head. "You'll have to work a little harder at it, that's all." His large, protruding nose slipped back into the business section of the paper. A financial advisor, he liked to keep abreast of the latest happenings.

Matt's eyes darted past the pool table to the new wooden shelf unit at the far end of the room. It was crammed with trophies, MVP plaques and medallions, brightly coloured ribbons and special awards. His father must have organized it while he was out.

Matt crossed the room for a closer inspection. His shoulders drooped as he neared the display. Almost everything belonged to his older brother, Kevin. Sure, Matt had gotten a few participation awards for playing soccer and T-Ball, when he was younger. But he'd never actually won a trophy. All the best ones were Kevin's. They were the ones his dad had placed at the front for everyone to see.

Matt glanced at his father stretched out on the chair, nose still buried in the newspaper. Maybe if he'd won the game, or if he'd gotten a lot of hits like Kevin usually did, then his dad might have been more interested in talking about it. Maybe if he was as good as Kevin, his father might make it out to more of his games.

Matt traced the finest trophy on the shelf with his fingers. He'd give just about anything, he decided, to win something special for the new display case, something to make his father really proud.

"Fat chance of that happening now," he murmured. Now that Spike McGarrity had come to town he could forget about winning anything. He glanced over to see if his father had heard him. Little movement came from the chair, just the quiet rustle of paper.

Matt turned his back on the trophy case, on the family room, and on his father. Slowly, he climbed the stairs.

What now? Matt wondered. There was nothing good on TV. He checked the pantry cupboards but there was nothing good to eat either. Ever since his mom had started her latest diet, cookies, chips, pop — all the essentials — had virtually disappeared from the Tucker household. "Think celery," she had posted on the fridge. Well, Matt couldn't make himself "think celery" no matter how hard he tried.

He plodded up the ornate wooden staircase to the landing above, then turned and slowly, dejectedly, made his way down the plushly carpeted hallway to his bedroom. He stood in the doorway for a moment, silently sizing up the possibilities.

He didn't feel like cleaning his lizard aquarium, looking at sports cards, or even playing video games. Most of the other things scattered about his room just didn't excite him anymore. All his friends had gotten rid of their junk ages ago — the dinky cars, superhero figurines, plastic dinosaurs, action figures. His father kept telling him to clear it out, but for some reason he just couldn't bring himself to part with any of it.

With nothing else to do, Matt finally decided to work on his research project. A faint smile suddenly turned up the corners of his mouth. Now there was something he could do better than his brother! The smile broadened into a self-satisfied grin. Matt always got higher marks at school.

"The amazing world of sharks," he said to himself as he settled in at his desk.

Matt's interest in sharks had grown ever since he had made the East City Sharks, Peterborough's peewee rep fastball team. It had seemed the obvious choice when Mrs. MacDonald, his eighth grade teacher, had let the class select their own topics for their final projects. At least until today.

Today, Matt couldn't concentrate. Thinking about sharks made him think about the team, about Spike McGarrity and the Lions winning the County Championship and about how he'd be disappointing his father once again.

Matt scribbled furiously on the clean sheet of paper in front of him. He scrunched it into a tight ball and fired it hard across the hall against the door of Kevin's bedroom. The Sharks were going to have to do something about that Spike McGarrity!

# 3

## Sabotage!

We could put itching powder on the ball," Ben suggested. "It would drive him crazy."

"There's no such thing," Matt blurted.

"How do you know?" Ben asked. "There might be. You don't know everything!"

"That's a stupid idea anyway," added Chris, the left-handed pitcher. He scowled intently. "You'd be hurting your own pitchers too!"

"How about ants in his pants?" offered Ryan Byrd. "That would really shake him up." He grabbed his waist, swivelled his hips, then pranced around as if he was some sort of cross between Elvis Presley, Michael Jackson, and a hyperactive grasshopper.

Ryan was the Sharks' shortstop. He had made the team last year, even though he'd played only a little organized ball. He had good hands, a strong arm, and was like lightning on the base paths. He was a bit crazy too, but a whole lot of fun and everyone on the team liked him a lot.

A few of the Sharks had hung around after their regular Tuesday night practice. The talk had turned to Spike McGarrity and possible ways to sabotage his pitching.

Kate, who up to this point had been listening intently to the others, suddenly giggled loudly. "I've got it!" she cried. "We could put laxatives in his water bottle!" She had seen an advertisement for laxatives on TV the night before. "He'd have to keep leaving the game, to run to the portable toilet at the far end of the field. They'd put in their second pitcher, and he's half Spike's speed. Why, the balls would seem like watermelons floating across the plate." She stroked both arms through mid-air, then raised them dramatically above her head in triumph, as if she'd smacked a homer. "We'd cream 'em."

The others laughed heartily.

"Too bad we couldn't rig up some kind of remote control system," Steve Hutton suggested. The second baseman's father was a research scientist and Steve had inherited his dad's enthusiasm for a good brainstorming session. "We could control the ball from the bench and walk everybody on the team. Or ..." He rubbed his chin thoughtfully.

"Or give ourselves all changeups," Chris said. "Only we'd be ready for them. Spike wouldn't catch us falling all over ourselves like last time."

"Like you do whenever you see Ryan's sister walk by," Matt teased. He'd never understand why Chris was so crazy about girls. Big waste of time, as far as he could see. Except Kate, of course. She could play a decent game of catch, or ride a bike like a maniac, just like any one of the guys. But he'd rather die than hold her hand or any of that other stuff. He just couldn't see what the big attraction was.

Mike Freeburn flipped off his cap and scratched his blond head. "I wish Spike would come down with the chicken pox or something, like I did last month. What a pain! I had to stay home for eight days. Missed two ball games and Ryan's birthday party." Suddenly, his face brightened. "And five days of school."

Everyone cheered.

"No, really." The tall stocky right-hander scratched his head again. "Does anybody know anyone with the chicken pox? If Spike could somehow catch the chicken pox right before our next game ..."

"Maybe we should just break his arm," Matt injected bluntly.

The rest of the Sharks turned incredulous eyes toward Matt, silenced by the serious tone in his voice.

"Just kidding," he said, grinning sheepishly. Deep down inside, however, Matt realized that he, for one, would be thrilled if that very thing happened. That would take care of Spike McGarrity!

The Sharks gradually began to drift homeward. The sinking sun had finally disappeared behind the new apartment complex across from the park, casting long dark shadows over the ball diamond. Dusk was rapidly descending and Matt had been given strict instructions to be home before dark.

Matt and Ben exited the park together, tossing a tennis ball back and forth as they meandered up the street.

Ben, the taller of the two, had thick dark hair, dark skin, and big brown eyes. He lived on Elmdale Crescent, only a few blocks past the Tuckers' house. He and Matt had been friends ever since they'd met in first grade at Queen Elizabeth Public School. Both shared the same love of sports and both excelled at school, although Matt usually had to work a little harder at it than Ben. Matt always figured Ben was one of the lucky ones. Everything seemed to come easy for him.

"We could do it, you know," Matt said, smacking the ball hard into his well-worn mitt and breaking into an easy jog to catch up to his friend.

"Are you crazy?" Ben asked. His face wore a look of disgust. "Break his arm? Are you nuts? We'd be in major trouble. I don't —"

"No, I didn't mean that. We could probably come up with something that would work, though," Matt continued. His eyes widened and he gestured frantically, excitement in his voice. "Something to get Spike out of the game. If we win all our other games, we'd only need to beat the Lions a couple of times. Then we'd be on our way to the Championship. All we need to do is come up with a couple of good ideas to keep Spike McGarrity out of the lineup whenever the Lions meet the Sharks ..."

Matt's voice trailed off breathlessly, but his mind raced on. Could they actually pull something like this off? He had read about things like this in books, and had seen them on TV and at the movies. Why couldn't it work for Matt, Ben, and the Sharks in real life? Why not?

The two boys quickened their pace. Although the soft glow from the streetlights overhead helped to illuminate the growing darkness, they could feel the chill in the night air. Matt shivered, not so much from the sharp bite in the late spring air, but from the thought of actually implementing such a plan. It sent strange, wonderful, tingling sensations up and down his spine. For the first time that week he was looking forward to playing ball.

"You're joking, aren't you?" Ben asked hopefully, glancing down at his friend's face as they arrived at the edge of Matt's driveway. The glow from the lamp above gave Matt an eerie, almost frightening appearance.

"I'm dead serious," Matt said.

"More like dead meat," Ben retorted. "Your father would have a major cow if he ever caught you doing something like that. I can just see it in the sports section of the *Examiner* ... 'Shark Trampled by Large Bovine.' "

Matt wasn't listening to Ben's banter. Nor did he notice the darkness that had suddenly blanketed Peterborough. His mind was focused. "You'll help, won't you?" he asked. "We just need to come up with a plan of attack!"

Ben moaned. "I'm not so sure I like the sound of this."

"All we need to do is figure out a few minor details." Matt briskly rubbed both hands together as he spoke. "The Lions can kiss that Championship goodbye."

# 4

# Trouble

Y ou're late!" Mr. Tucker was at the back door, hands planted firmly on his hips, eyebrows knitted into a fierce frown. "I said home before dark." His voice was loud and cold; his face flushed. "You're going to be punished for this!"

"But it just got dark this very minute," Matt protested. "We could still see. All the others just went home!"

"I don't care about the others! You know the rules!"

A slight blond woman suddenly appeared in the kitchen doorway. She had the same friendly blue eyes as Matt, the same round face and tiny circular chin, and the same way of using her hands when she spoke. Matt had been told several times that he resembled his mother, but lately it was happening more frequently. The fact that they were almost the same height made their similarities stand out even more.

Marg Tucker lightly placed a hand on her husband's arm. "Don't be too hard on him, John," she pleaded. "He's usually pretty good at getting home on time."

"Rules are rules!" Matt's father furiously wagged his finger close to his son's nose. "They're not meant to be broken." He turned to face his wife. "And have you taken a look at that room of his lately? It's gotten totally out of hand. I want him straight home after school tomorrow and in his room until dinner." Suddenly, he pivoted sharply on one heel and pointed to the stairs. "In fact, you might as well march on up there right now, young man. It's almost bedtime anyway."

"Kevin's not home yet," Matt stated defiantly, angrily slamming his glove to the floor.

His mom flashed him a warning look.

"Kevin's older than you — two years older." Mr. Tucker's face was red, purplish veins stood out all around his neck. "You know that as well as I do," he shouted.

"One and a half," Matt added meekly, moving farther away from his father.

Mr. Tucker inhaled deeply and pointed once again in the direction of the stairs.

A lump was beginning to form in Matt's throat. He and Ben had plans for after school tomorrow. At least Matt did; he had plans enough for both of them. He had been turning them over in his mind on his way up the walk.

Matt swallowed. He felt like crying, but he choked back the tears. If he let himself cry, his father would surely call him a baby. Instead, he stomped up the stairs, loud enough to let his father know he wasn't pleased, but not quite loud enough to make his father any angrier. It had taken several previous attempts, but Matt had finally figured out the difference.

Matt flopped onto his bed. Minou was already there, giving herself a leisurely bath by the side of his pillow. He sank his fingers into the cat's soft grey fur and cuddled the small warm bundle close to his face.

It wasn't fair! Nothing was fair! Kevin was always getting the best of everything, just because he was a little older. Matt was a teenager too! His mom had given him his own deodorant on the day of his thirteenth birthday. She had said he was going to have to start wearing it every day, and taking daily showers and all the other things that grownups did. He hadn't been looking forward to it, but it did mean he was growing up, didn't it? And it really hadn't been that bad after all.

His father didn't need to keep treating him like he was some little kid, especially after the talk he had given him. Even though Matt already knew all about that sex stuff from watching TV and listening to the kids at school, his father had wanted to make sure.

Matt rolled over, gently pulled Minou onto his chest and sighed heavily. He really should have known better. His dad was obsessed about not walking around town after dark, but he'd been thinking about Spike and had forgotten all about his stupid curfew. Ben had been no help. He hadn't been in any hurry to get home. He wouldn't be grounded. His parents had fewer rules, and they always stretched or ignored the few they did have.

Oh, how Matt wished his father was more like Mr. Aoki, with his easy laugh and quick warm smile. He wished his father loved him as much as Mr. Aoki loved Ben, or even as much as he loved his older brother, Kevin.

Matt stroked Minou over and over again. The softness of her fur and the warmth from her body was comforting. Purring contentedly, Minou focused her bright yellow eyes on Matt's face. She kneaded her slim pussy willow paws into his heaving chest. Matt smiled. He had read somewhere that cats did that when they were really pleased or wanted to show affection. It felt good to know that at least somebody loved him, even if it was only a cat.

Well, he'd show his dad he was just as good as Kevin. He'd show that Spike McGarrity too. He'd show them all!

# 5

# Ditto

Y ou're really serious about this, aren't you?" Ben called loudly over his shoulder as he and Matt pedalled toward the ballpark a few days later.

East City Bowl was only a short bicycle ride away, and yet it boasted the finest softball diamond in Peterborough. The playing field was situated on a plain a short distance above the Otonabee River. Several bleachers and rock gardens had been carved out of the surrounding hillsides, reminding Matt of the ancient Greek amphitheatres they had talked about in English class.

Today, the diamond had been freshly lined and graded, the sun was shining, the sky a brilliant blue. A light breeze was stirring the leaves of nearby trees. It would be a perfect evening for a ball game. Matt, totally oblivious to the beauty of his surroundings, leaned his bike against the chain link fence.

"I thought you might have forgotten about Spike by now," Ben added.

"I'm not going to forget him," Matt said determinedly. His voice was calm and steady, but his eyes lacked their usual warmth and playfulness. "I'm not going to stand around and let this new kid spoil our season. This was supposed to be our year, remember?"

"Aren't you guys planning on playing tonight?" Coach Leahy was growing impatient.

Matt nodded at the coach. He suddenly realized that he and Ben were already ten minutes late and now they were standing by the fence, chatting nonchalantly, as if they had time to spare.

The two boys quickly moved to the bench area and laced up their cleats. Matt played an easy game of catch with Ben, then, after Ben left to warm up the pitchers, he joined another group for a quick game of pepper.

Kate Crowley took the bat first, hitting sharp short grounders to the others who were gathered in a semicircle about fifteen feet in front of her. Matt had found the drill difficult when he first joined the team, but lately his reaction time had improved immensely. Very rarely did he let one slip by.

Until tonight.

"That's the third time in a row you've screwed up," Steve Hutton scolded. "If you don't watch out you'll be riding the pine."

"Might as well be on the bench. We're going nowhere. Nobody's going to get by the Lions with Spi —"

"We're not playing the Lions tonight; we're playing the Hornets," Kate reminded Matt with a toss of her auburn head. "And Steve's right," she admonished. "I saw Coach glancing over here a minute ago and there was a mega frown on his face. Why don't you just forget about Spike and —"

Kate's warning came too late.

"Concentrate," Coach yelled as a sharp sizzler zipped past Matt into the grassy outfield. "Wake up over there! You've got to keep your eye on the ball. Watch it come right off the bat."

Matt's eyes turned to focus on the bat in Kate's hand. But his mind stayed focused on Spike even after Coach sent him to the outfield to shag a few fly balls. Figuring out a plan of attack was proving to be more difficult than he had anticipated.

Suddenly, out of the corner of his eye, he caught sight of a fly ball soaring in his direction. He sidestepped to the left and frantically thrust his glove into midair. His timing was terrible. The ball rolled all the way to the fence.

"Come on, Matt!" hollered Mr. Crowley, the assistant coach. "Get your body behind the ball. You know better than that."

Matt's face reddened. He shouldn't have missed an easy one like that.

Once the game got underway, Matt's performance echoed his warm-up play. In fact, the entire team struggled. Normally the Sharks could defeat the Hornets with runs to spare. Tonight, however, they eeked out a meagre one-run victory in the bottom of the seventh.

# 6

## Oh Brother!

The Amazing World of Sharks, Matt pencilled lightly on the cover page of his research project.

"Yeah, right," he muttered. "Truly amazing." He felt like chucking the whole lot into the garbage, or better yet, running it through one of those paper shredding machines at his father's office and mincing it into tiny useless bits.

Who cares if there are more than three hundred kinds of sharks in the world, he thought, hastily flipping through the notes he had scrawled on his file cards. Who cares if the dwarf shark is only six inches long while the whale shark can measure up to sixty feet? Who cares if more people die each year from bee stings than shark attacks? Or if a shark once lived that had jaws so big you could drive a small car through them? Facts that had once excited and intrigued him now seemed dry and boring.

The East City Sharks were doomed to defeat, washed up like the carcass of a beached whale shark rotting in the sun. Matt could care less about sharks of any kind. He wished he could change the title on his project and start all over again.

"But, it's too late now," he sighed. The projects were due in less than a week.

He pursed his lips, hunched his narrow shoulders over the small wooden desk and began to doodle furiously on a blank index card.

"How'd you guys do today?" Kevin Tucker's dark handsome frame almost filled Matt's bedroom doorway. "Win your game?"

"Barely," Matt said flatly. "The final score was five to four. Ryan hit a two-run double in the bottom of the seventh."

"You guys might as well pack it in and hang up your cleats and gloves if you can barely get by the Hornets. How are you going to handle Spike McGarrity and the Lions? That kid's supposed to be something else, from what I've heard," Kevin continued, checking his profile in the mirror as he entered the room. He rubbed at the small red zit protruding from his chin, then raised his thick brows quizzically. "Is he really as good as everyone's been saying?"

"He's super fast," Matt said, frowning deeply. "I bet you couldn't even hit him," he added, a slight smile playing about his lips as he spoke.

"Yeah, right!" Kevin replied cockily. "You're talking to the Bantam Batting King, remember. I could hit that little twerp, no problem."

Kevin was right, Matt admitted to himself with a sting of jealousy. The all-star teams had recently posted stats in *The Peterborough Examiner*. Kevin Tucker had been the number one hitter for the bantam squad with a whopping .662 batting average. His coach was already comparing him to Marty Kernaghan, some guy he knew who'd started playing squirt softball in the small village of Grafton, then gone on to become All-Canadian and All-World MVP. No wonder Kevin thought he was so hot.

Matt sighed heavily. Kevin would probably receive another gigantic trophy for winning the batting title this year. He might even be his team's MVP again — he was one of their best pitchers. In fact, Peterborough's bantams might go all the way and win the Championship. They'd get their pictures in the *Examiner*, new jackets, likely even a ride through town on the back of a bright red fire engine.

"Maybe I could help," Kevin offered. "Give you a little extra batting practice or something." Bending intently over the desk, he studied Matt's cartoon sketch. "You know, this is really pretty good. Why don't you put a few of these in your project? Teachers eat that kind of stuff up. Bonus marks for extra work and all that."

"What would you know about bonus marks?" Matt chided. "You're so stupid, it's all you can do to get a passing gr —"

As soon as the words had left his mouth, Matt wished he could bite them back. He could almost picture them floating through the air in slow motion while he groped futilely at them, trying to catch them before they landed on his brother's ears. He hadn't really meant to be so mean. The words had just sort of spurted out before he'd had a chance to even think about what he was saying. After all, Kevin was only tr —

"Yeow!" yelped Matt. A sharp stab of pain surged through the back of his neck as Kevin thrust one of his elbows into the side of his head.

"I was only trying to help, you little punk," Kevin shouted, grabbing Matt's raised arm in a tight hold. "Why do you have to be such a little jerk about everything?" He released his grip and spun around to leave the room.

Leaping out of his chair, Matt rushed at his older brother, head down, a battering ram, long thin arms flailing.

"Leave me alone," he cried. "Get out of my room and leave me alone." His eyes snapped angrily. "I wouldn't want your help. Not in a million years! Not even if you were the best pitcher in the entire world!"

Kevin gave his younger brother a hard shove onto the bed.

"You're crazy," he said, shrugging his broad shoulders with exaggerated indifference. "If that's the way you want it — fine. But don't you ask me to help you with anything ever again. Do you hear me?"

"I hear you," Matt shouted, jumping to his feet as he watched Kevin strut out of the room. "I don't need your help!" He tossed his blond head defiantly. "I don't need anyone's help. I can take care of Spike McGarrity all by myself!"

# 7

# Brain Wave

Spike McGarrity's reputation spread throughout the county with the speed of an infectious disease. Everyone was talking about the new kid with the incredible fastball, the wicked changeup, the impeccable control.

At Queen Elizabeth the following Monday, a group of third grade girls were skipping on the paved area adjacent to the primary yard.

> Spike McGarrity,
> Mean and swift,
> How many batters can he whiff?

Matt watched the rope turners pick up speed while Steve Hutton's little sister, Nichola, jumped up and down, up and down, the others chanting frantically, "Two, four, six, eight ..."

Matt scowled. He had never spoken two words to this Spike kid, but everywhere he went, he was there, trailing him like some pesky varmint in a Saturday morning cartoon.

Well, he'd had enough! He would definitely have to come up with a plan. That's all there was to it. But, it would have to be something so incredibly ingenious, so inconspicuous ... it would have to be something absolutely foolproof.

Matt's mind stayed focused on Spike for most of the week. He thought about Spike while he ate, dreamed about him when he slept. He thought about him during the Sharks' game against the Bears, and made two unfortunate errors in centre field, almost costing the Sharks the game. Spike McGarrity was even on Matt's mind while he worked on his school report.

Sprinkling a few cartoons throughout the project had been a good idea, he had finally admitted. A great idea, in fact, for it had renewed his interest in sharks and given his notes extra spark and vitality.

Matt added a drawing when he wrote about the infrequent occurrence of shark attacks.

Why wasn't the girl afraid of the shark?

It was a man-eating shark.

He added a couple more when he talked about the many different types of sharks.

By Friday morning, *The Amazing World of Sharks* was complete. Matt sat at his desk stroking the brilliant blue booklet cover in admiration. This was his best project ever. Thanks to Kevin, he admitted reluctantly.

What would happen if you brought a whale shark home?

Your parents would raise the roof.

A puzzled expression suddenly creased his brow. Kevin. He was becoming more and more confused about him. Sometimes, Matt had to admit, he felt really proud of his older brother. Other times he wished Kevin had never been born. Everything had been much simpler when he was younger. His mom and dad, especially his dad, just didn't seem to understand anything anymore.

As for Spike McGarrity and formulating a plan of attack, well, the week had been a total write-off. Matt had gotten nowhere.

* * *

"These cartoons are simply wonderful," Mrs. MacDonald complimented as she scanned Matt's report later that morning. "They're so well done." She made the same strange clucking sound she always made when she was extremely pleased with something.

"Thank you," Matt murmured.

What type of shark should you never tell a secret to?

A megamouth.

"Why don't you take these down to Mr. Baldwin? He'd love to see them, I'm sure. He's always interested in the special talents of the students in his school."

Two minutes later, Matt gently knocked on the door of the principal's office.

"Come on in. He'll be with you in a minute," the secretary said. She glanced up at Matt, her slim fingers flying over the computer keyboard. "He's just finishing up with a parent. I'm sure it won't take long." She motioned for Matt to take a seat.

"That's okay," Matt said. "I'll wait outside."

Matt leaned against the wall to the right of the office doorway and stared down at his feet. He didn't seem to be growing much, but they sure were, every day it seemed. He could feel his toes pushing against the ends of his sneakers even now. But he wasn't going to tell his mom, not for a while anyway. A larger pair would only make him look like one of those floppy-footed circus clo —

A loud, resounding ring suddenly broke into Matt's thoughts. It was the phone on the secretary's desk. Just as Mrs. Moritz answered the call, it hit ... instant inspiration. Matt gasped and his eyes grew wide. Why, that was it! It was too easy. That had been the problem all along. The answer was so easy it had eluded him. He had been trying to concoct something wonderfully weird and complicated, when all he had to do to keep Spike out of the game was make a phone call, a simple phone call. How could he have been so stupid?

Next time the Sharks met the Lions, he would call Spike a couple hours before game time and relay the message that the game had been delayed. By the time Spike arrived at the park, it would be too late. The game would be over with the Sharks, no doubt, victorious. It was easy. It was foolproof. It was the perfect plan of attack.

Matt stood motionless for a few seconds, smiling, relishing the moment. Then he grinned broadly, tucked his project under his arm and strolled off down the long narrow hallway. Forget about the principal. Forget about sharks. Bring on Spike McGarrity and the Lakefield Lions!

# 8

# Plan of Attack!

I think you're crazy!" Ben exclaimed. "You've totally lost your mind."

"Aw, come on," Matt pleaded. "I've helped you with lots of things."

"Yeah, right. Name one."

"Well …"

"Better yet. Name one good reason why I should help you."

"You're my best friend."

"I was your best friend."

Matt's voice softened. "Look, it's not a big deal. Spike's parents will probably be driving him to the game, right?"

Ben nodded.

"They never miss a game," Matt continued. "They think their kid's Darren Zack, maybe even the next Ray Judd."

"What's your point?"

Matt smiled smugly. "It's perfect. Don't you see? No one will get a chance to straighten him out about the game time. And he's new in town. He won't recognize everyone's voice on his team. He'll just think I'm one of the guys." Matt's blue eyes sparkled mischievously. "All I need is someone to help me work out a few possible scenarios. I don't want to sound like a blithering idiot when I get on the phone."

Ben remained silent a moment, a dubious expression on his dark round face. He scratched his head thoughtfully, then finally, reluctantly, he conceded. "Okay, okay. I'll help you tonight. But," he added firmly, his brown eyes piercing, "you're totally on your own tomorrow when you actually try and pull this thing off."

Ben spent a couple of hours role-playing with Matt. Initially, he was tentative, but after a while Ben warmed up to the task. Before long the two were enjoying themselves immensely. Every few minutes howls of laughter would erupt from behind the door of Matt's bedroom.

Eventually Matt was satisfied. As far as he was concerned, he had all the bases covered. Whether Spike answered the phone, or his mother, brother, father or even his grandmother, Matt was prepared. He had an answer to every question a McGarrity might pose, a solution to any problem that might present itself.

What's more, he could make the call from the privacy of his own bedroom. His grandmother had given both Tucker boys their own phones the previous Christmas.

"That's what grandparents are for," Grandma had said, laughing heartily. "To spoil the grandchildren."

She had given them massive packs of ick 'em stick 'em two Christmases ago, the same slimy goop Mr. Tucker had previously outlawed from the house, after Matt and Kevin had left little dark smudge marks all over the living room ceiling.

Dad had kept quiet about it until after Grandma had left. Then he had insisted they throw the gooey green stuff into the garbage.

The phones had been an entirely different matter. Matt had never seen his parents so displeased with Grandma. Finally, however, they had given in. The boys could keep the phones, they decided, but with one stipulation: no more major presents from Grandma without consulting them first.

* * *

Matt hurried home from school the following afternoon. Immediately, he climbed the stairs to his bedroom. "Lots of homework," he called to his mom in the family room. Then, afraid that his enthusiasm for homework would cause suspicion, he went back down to the kitchen. He would grab a bite to eat first.

Matt opened the fridge door and surveyed the contents. A miniature pink pig squealed, "Oink, oink, oink," as soon as the refrigerator light flashed on. It was Marg Tucker's latest dieting device. Matt grabbed a couple of apples, then shut the door. He opened and closed it one more time just to hear the oinking piece of plastic.

Why was he so nervous? he wondered, once again climbing the stairs. It was going to be easy, but for some reason he could feel strange flutterings in the pit of his stomach. Matt drew in a long, deep breath. He let it out slowly as he approached the phone.

"Don't quit now," he told himself. He inhaled again, then glanced around furtively, like a spy about to embark on a top-secret mission. The door of the bedroom was shut tightly. There was no sound of approaching footsteps, just the quiet purring of Minou who was curled up in one corner of the bed. Matt began to dial the number he had obtained from information the day before.

A soft feminine voice answered on the other end of the line. "Hello?" she said.

"Hello," Matt replied, his voice cracking slightly. His voice had been acting funny lately. Please not tonight, he pleaded. "Is Spike there?" he queried nervously as he crossed his fingers. With any luck, the response would be negative. It would be a lot easier to simply leave the message.

"Yes, he's right here," the woman said.

Matt braced himself.

"Hello?"

The friendliness of the voice startled Matt and he hesitated a moment before proceeding. "Umm, just called to let you know our game tonight against the Sharks has been moved back a couple of hours. We'll be playing at eight o'clock instead of six."

"Really," Spike said. "How come?"

Matt's voice did not falter. He and Ben had rehearsed this very scene. "Some scheduling problem, I guess. Coach wanted me to give everyone a call."

"We might get to play under the lights then. That'll be great. We don't get to do that too often."

Seems like a nice enough guy, Matt decided, after quickly hanging up the phone. Not at all like the villain he had constructed in his imagination.

Matt flung himself onto his bed and stretched out from head to toe, easing the tension from his body. He could relax now. The hard part was over. He had even managed to get off the line before Spike had thought to ask who was calling. Everything had gone according to plan.

Minou strolled toward Matt, climbed onto his chest, and began to circle. Finally, she settled down on top of him, again kneading her paws against his body.

"Easy," Matt whispered to Minou as he rubbed the thick grey fur. Just as he'd figured.

Minou's ears twitched ever so slightly, almost as if she understood that Matt was speaking to her. "Just you wait and see," he added confidently. "Now the game will be easy too."

# 9

# Caught

Before the rest of the Tuckers arrived home for dinner, Coach Leahy had called Matt. He often invited players to the park thirty minutes early for a little extra help. Ben and Steve Hutton had gone the previous week to practice tagging runners out at second.

No wonder Coach had called him tonight, Matt figured. He'd been struggling lately, both defensively and at the plate.

Matt didn't have time to wait for dinner. He wolfed down a couple micro-wrinkled hot dogs, quickly dressed for the game, then hopped on his bike.

He zoomed past Mr. Meldrum spray-painting a new picket fence at the end of the street, and a group of young ponytailed girls around the next corner playing hopscotch. Matt veered toward them, then swerved away at the last second, leaving a flurry of shrieks and squeals behind.

As he drew near the park, he noticed Coach Leahy was alone. The coach had meticulously laid out the team's equipment on the home side of the diamond: bats along the back of the screen arranged neatly, batting helmets carefully placed right below. Next he had set the jug of water on the edge of the bench. When he raised his head, he spotted Matt. Coach's eyes did not light up in recognition the way they usually did, as Matt had expected.

"You're the only one I asked to come early tonight," Coach stated. He waved one hand in the direction of the bench. "Sit down, Matt. We need to talk."

Did Coach know something? Matt wondered, his face reddening. How could he? Ben would never tell. He must be upset with how he'd been playing lately.

"I've been talking to the Lions' coach," Coach Leahy continued, his tone growing graver. "Seems somebody was trying to prevent Spike from taking the mound tonight."

Matt lowered his blue eyes sheepishly.

"I know all about it, Matt."

"How did —"

Coach cut him off. "That's not the issue here. Why would you do such a thing?"

"I … I don't know," Matt stammered. He could feel a lump in the back of his throat growing larger, moisture welling up around his eyes. He blinked rapidly, then squeezed his eyes tight hoping to build a dam against the encroaching tears.

"Take your time," Coach said, lowering himself to the bench beside Matt and glancing at his watch. "No one will be here for quite a while. I just want to get to the bottom of this."

"I guess … I guess I just wanted to win," Matt finally admitted, breaking the awkward silence that had grown between them.

"We all want to win," Coach replied sternly, "but we're not going to start lying and cheating in order to do it. Wouldn't mean much then, now would it?"

Several tears began to slowly make their way down Matt's flushed cheeks. "Kevin's always winning," he said sadly. "He's a lot better than me. Everybody likes to watch him play. They don't care much about watching me."

"I have noticed your parents haven't made it out to many games. I just figured they were busy working or something."

Matt paused for a moment and brushed the tears aside. "Dad never misses my brother Kevin's games. He's the best hitter on his team. The best pitcher, too. Everybody likes him better," he suddenly blurted, "just because he's so good at everything."

Coach's eyes brightened. He reached over and placed an arm around Matt's shoulder. "This isn't about Spike at all, is it?" His voice had mellowed.

Matt did not answer, but the tightness he had been feeling inside began to loosen as he let the tears stream down his face.

Coach smiled at Matt. "I think I'm beginning to understand why you did this." He offered Matt one of the small white towels from the first aid kit. Matt wiped his face while Coach continued, his tone once again becoming serious. "It still doesn't make it right, though. I'm going to have to sit you out of the game tonight. And I think the league will probably take some kind of disciplinary action. The Lions' coach was pretty upset. There might be a short suspension."

Coach's smile broadened. "Look, son. I made you one of the team's captains because I liked your aggressiveness and determination — your desire to win." He chuckled quietly. "But this isn't exactly what I had in mind."

A slight smile creased the corners of Matt's mouth in response. Quickly, it disappeared. "You're not going to tell my father about this, are you?" Matt's blue eyes were pleading.

"I think this might be the perfect time to have a talk with your parents."

# 10

# Take Me Out of the Ball Game

Matt sat glumly on the end of the bench, watching as Coach Leahy adjusted the lineup for the game.

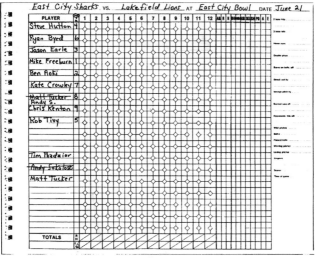

| PLAYER | POS | 1 | 2 | 3 | 4 | 5 | 6 | 7 | 8 | 9 | 10 | 11 | 12 | AB | R | H |
|--------|-----|---|---|---|---|---|---|---|---|---|----|----|----|----|----|----|
| Steve Hutton | 4 | | | | | | | | | | | | | | | |
| Ryan Byrd | 6 | | | | | | | | | | | | | | | |
| Jason Earle | 3 | | | | | | | | | | | | | | | |
| Mike Freeburn | 1 | | | | | | | | | | | | | | | |
| Ben Aoki | 2 | | | | | | | | | | | | | | | |
| Kate Crowley | 7 | | | | | | | | | | | | | | | |
| Matt Tucker / Andy S. | 8 | | | | | | | | | | | | | | | |
| Chris Kenton | 9 | | | | | | | | | | | | | | | |
| Rob Tivy | 5 | | | | | | | | | | | | | | | |
| | | | | | | | | | | | | | | | | |
| | | | | | | | | | | | | | | | | |
| Tim Radzior | | | | | | | | | | | | | | | | |
| Andy Sokolow | | | | | | | | | | | | | | | | |
| Matt Tucker | | | | | | | | | | | | | | | | |
| | | | | | | | | | | | | | | | | |
| | | | | | | | | | | | | | | | | |
| | | | | | | | | | | | | | | | | |
| TOTALS | | | | | | | | | | | | | | | | |

Coach handed the scorebook over to Matt. "You can get Lakefield's lineup while I help finish the warm-ups and talk to the rest of the team. They'll need to know what's happened." He tugged at the peak of his cap, pulling it forward to cover his receding hair line. "I've tried to keep this thing quiet, but the Lakefield team seems to know all about it. Our team might as well hear it from me."

Matt waited for the opposing bench area to clear before he made his way to the Lakefield side of the screen. He could feel the gaze of the parents and players; he could hear the whispers behind his back, and see the fingers trying to discreetly point in his direction. Coach was right. Everyone on the Lions' side seemed to know all about the phone fiasco. How did they find out it was him? he wondered once again.

To make matters worse, the Lions were all wearing new gold and black uniforms and sporting expensive hats with the letter *L* emblazoned across the front. They had arrived carrying matching equipment bags for their cleats and gloves. The coaches and manager were decked out too, in matching warm-up suits.

Planning on looking pretty sharp for the County Championships, Matt figured, a sharp stab of envy adding to his humiliation. He plunked himself down beside the manager and filled in the Lions' roster.

"Coaches and captains!" bellowed the umpire, as Matt returned to the Sharks' side of the diamond.

Matt glanced over at Coach Leahy. He was assigning Ben to replace him for the customary meeting and handshakes at home plate.

"My life is over," Matt whispered quietly to himself. Before long, every one in town would know what a jerk he'd been.

The Sharks took the field first. Third baseman, Rob Flamminio, led off for the Lions. The long lean infielder worked the count to three and two, then walked. The next two batters popped out and it looked like the Sharks might escape the inning unscathed, until Spike, batting cleanup, ripped a hard blast down the first base line to score Rob. The Lions led one to nothing.

During the second half of the inning, the Sharks went down in order. Steve Hutton, Ryan Byrd, and Jason Earle all struck out: Steve and Ryan on three straight fastballs, Jason on an incredible knuckleball changeup.

The pattern continued for much of the game, the Lions scratching out a run or two here and there, the Sharks remaining scoreless.

"Might as well be on the bench," Matt grumbled to himself. "Nobody's going to hit this guy."

"Hustle on out there." Coach Leahy slapped Ben encouragingly on the back. "Play tight defence," he called. "It ain't over 'til it's over!"

Spike's changeup was amazing, Matt admitted to himself a few innings later. He hadn't seen anything like it since Ron Rupp, the pitcher for the California Cuties, had been in town for Kevin's team's fundraiser two years before. Combined with that awesome speed, it was no wonder the batters were helpless.

Matt sat quietly on the bench listening to the chatter of the Lions.

> Rob, Rob, he's our man.
> If he can't do it,
> Spike can.
> Spike, Spike, he's our man.
> If he can't do it,
> NO ONE CAN!

He felt like covering his ears, like he used to when he was a little kid and wanted to block out his father's yelling. But, it would have been pointless. The Lions' noisy barrage continued.

> Fans, fans, in the stands,
> If you're with us clap your hands.

The families and friends of the Lions on the opposite side of the diamond cheerfully obliged.

> Fans, fans, in your seats,
> If you're with us stamp your feet.

The bleachers rocked in rhythm. Then,

> Lions, Lions,
> Hear us roar.
> Let's beat those Sharks.
> Let's score, score, score!

Ben squeezed onto the end of the bench beside Matt.

"Diarrhea," he stated matter of factly, as if he was some kind of play-by-play announcer. "Verbal diarrhea." He laughed a dull sarcastic laugh. "The whole team's got it. It just keeps coming and coming, spewing out of their mouths virtually nonstop."

"My life is definitely over," Matt repeated gloomily. He hadn't heard a word of his friend's chatter. He pointed in the direction of the upper gate. Mr. and Mrs. Tucker were making their way down the concrete steps.

# 11

## Game Over

If anyone had asked him later, Matt could not have given an accurate account of the final few innings. He did not discover until the next day that the score had been eight to nothing in favour of the Lions.

After the arrival of his parents, Matt had been entirely consumed with dread. The post-game confrontation would no doubt be … he did not even want to consider the possibilities. His mind had gone numb. If only the game could go on forever, he thought. If only he had never come up with that stupid plan.

"Join the lineup, Matt," Coach instructed firmly. "You can shake hands with the rest of the team."

Matt kept his head lowered as he made his way down the expanse of gold and black. There were a few snickers, an odd remark, but he somehow managed to make it through. Ben had gone in front of him and had done his best to distract the Lions. Even so, it had been the most humiliating experience of his life.

Coach Leahy walked briskly to where Matt's parents were sitting behind the backstop. He escorted them to the far end of the bleachers out of earshot of the others.

Matt watched forlornly. Coach was probably giving them all the dirty details.

He stood in silence twenty minutes later while his dad loaded his bike into the back of the van. His father would not make a scene in front of everyone, Matt rationalized. Mr. Tucker would wait until the family was alone in the van, then he'd let Matt have it.

Never, in his wildest imaginings, could he have predicted what would happen next.

Mrs. Tucker turned around and faced her son as the van pulled under the concrete bridge below the parking lot. Her blue eyes were troubled. "We're sorry, Matt," she said quietly.

Matt's mouth gaped open. His nervous fidgeting stopped.

"Don't get us wrong here," Mr. Tucker interrupted. "We're not pleased with what you've done by any means. But Coach Leahy seems to think your situation at home may have played a big part in your behaviour." He stopped a moment later at the red light in front of the Quaker Oats office building. "At first I told Coach Leahy he was out of line." He glanced quickly at his wife. "But your mother insisted we hear him out."

Mrs. Tucker offered Matt a slight smile as her husband continued. "He feels you're jealous of Kevin, that maybe we give your older brother more attention than we give you. And that it somehow contributed to your behaviour."

"We haven't done it intentionally, Matt, if that's the case," his mom said, pointing toward the intersection. "The light's green, John," she added. "Do you really feel that way, Matt? That we prefer Kevin to you."

Matt did not respond at first. Finally, he nodded.

"We certainly love you both the same," his mom continued. "But I guess Coach Leahy is on to something. Sometimes it's easier for people on the outside to see things that are too close to the rest of us."

"I've gone to more of Kevin's games this year," Mr. Tucker admitted. "Maybe it's because he arrived on the scene first. I don't know. Maybe it's because he's the pitcher, and they're looking at him for the Ontario team. But, I really wasn't aware of it until your coach pointed it out."

"I'd never really thought about it too much before," Matt's mom interjected. "It must be tough to have an older brother who's the star on his team." She looked Matt directly in the eye and smiled. "We're proud of you too. You're doing really well." She chuckled lightly. "At least you were until this Spike thing started. And you've got abilities and talents in areas that Kevin doesn't. Your drawing, for example. I'd give anything to have a gift like that."

Matt's father shook his head from side to side. "I still can't fully comprehend why you'd do such a thing."

"You've certainly never done anything like this before," his mom added.

"I didn't believe it at first," his dad continued. "In fact, I asked the coach: How did they know it was you?"

"How *did* they know it was me?" Matt was feeling braver now and his curiosity was growing stronger with each passing hour.

"Call display," his father replied. "Our name and number flashed on the small screen on Spike's phone."

Matt's shoulders drooped heavily. How could he have been so stupid? Of course, call display. He had forgotten all about call display.

"When Spike got off the phone and had time to think about it," Mr. Tucker was saying, "he didn't remember any Tucker kid being on his team. He checked the roster, then called his coach to see what was up." The light was red again, and Mr. Tucker turned and faced his son. His voice was firm, his manner stern and controlled. "I'm not going to get mad and rant and rave, but you are going to be grounded for this and Coach Leahy thinks there'll be a short suspension, three games perhaps. Apparently, the McGarritys weren't that worried about it, but the Lions' Coach was pretty upset." Mr. Tucker paused for a moment, then added, almost as an after-thought, "And you'll be calling that pitcher," he stated firmly, "to apologize."

Oh, no, Matt winced. That's all he needed, more humili-ation. He stared blankly out the window as the van passed the corner store. They usually stopped for a pop or some ice cream whenever his parents drove him home from a game, but he figured he'd better not mention it. That might be pressing his luck a little too much.

"You're lucky they didn't throw you right out of the league," Mrs. Tucker added sternly. "What you did was pretty serious. You understand that, don't you?"

Matt nodded meekly.

"Coach didn't want us to be too hard on you," Mr. Tucker added. "He seems to think you've learned your lesson, that nothing like this will happen again."

"I think we've all learned something here," Matt's mom added, catching her husband's eye with a meaningful glance.

Matt remained thoughtful for the rest of the ride home. Coach had really stood up for him in front of his parents, and he'd brought something to their attention Matt would never have mentioned on his own. It was really amazing how much better he felt now that everything was actually out in the open. He was going to have to make it up to him, somehow. He'd show Coach that naming him captain hadn't been a mistake, after all. Why, school wasn't even out yet. There were still lots of games left on the schedule. He had the entire summer to turn this thing around.

# 12

# Back on Track

"Y ou're supposed to be the smart one," Matt reprimanded Ben jokingly. "Why didn't you think about call display?"

"I told you it was a crazy idea," Ben defended himself. "What more could I say?"

"I guess it was a stupid thing to do," Matt admitted.

"What did Spike say," Ben asked, "when you called to apologize?"

"Actually, he was pretty cool about it. Said it was no big deal. I think he was a little, umm … what's the word, ahh … you know…."

"Flattered," Ben blurted.

"Yeah, that's it."

"See," Ben added, laughing, "I am the smart one."

Matt giggled, despite the fact that he was grounded. He had wondered if his parents might remove the telephone from his room, but so far so good. He and Ben were on it constantly.

"Actually, we talked for quite a while. He's good because of all the practicing he does. He throws a hundred pitches almost every night. Then his dad helps him with his batting."

Matt continued thoughtfully, deliberately, as if it was hard to get the words to come out right. "I guess I was jealous or something. My father's always so busy. And it seems like he has more time for Kevin than me. I think it's 'cause Kevin's the oldest and he's so good at sports."

Again, Matt felt confused, both angry and proud at the same time. But this time it was different. The anger seemed diffused. Calmly, he continued. "I think things will be a little different, now that my mom and dad know how I was feeling. The whole thing seems almost too dumb to be real. It feels like it must have been part of a dream. I can't believe I actually tried to pull something that stupid."

"I bet we'd be good too," Ben said, "if we worked as hard as Spike."

Matt paused for a moment, considering the options. "You know, my dad is pretty busy, but I bet I could get Kevin to practice with us. When my grounding is over," he added. "I think Kevin's just as fast as Spike. We argued about it before. But I'm sure he'd help out now, if I asked."

"We could give each other batting practice too," Ben offered. "You know, into the back of the screen like we saw that coach do at our last tournament."

Matt's face assumed a look of stoic determination. "I bet if the whole team worked at it, we could beat those Lions — fair and square!"

# 13

---

# Shark Attack!

I've got it all figured out," Matt announced as Ben made his way down the stairs into the Tucker's family room. Matt gently scooted Minou off his chest and jumped to his feet. "Our next plan of attack," he continued. "I've got it all worked out."

Ben, who had dropped by the Tuckers' to watch some Saturday afternoon TV, suddenly looked alarmed.

"Don't worry. Don't worry," Matt assured him. "It's perfectly legit. I've been thinking about it all day. I was hoping you'd come by. I'm going to call our new plan — Shark Attack!"

"Slow down, slow down for a sec," Ben interrupted, throwing himself and his knapsack to the floor. "Let me have a turn. Don't you want to hear my good news?"

"Okay. Okay. What's up?" Matt asked impatiently, eager to spill out the details of his plan.

"Spike's going on vacation," Ben announced happily, sitting up on his elbows, a triumphant gleam in his big brown eyes. "In about a week, as soon as school is out for the summer. Steve's little sister goes to gymnastics with Spike's sister. That's how I found out." Ben continued excitedly. "He'll be away for at least two weeks from the sound of things. The Lions are bound to lose a few games when he's

gone. Maybe we'll finish in first place after all. Maybe we'll
advance to the Championships without a plan."

Matt's blue eyes danced with delight. He sat down on the
floor beside his friend. "You're right! It is great news. In fact,
it makes Shark Attack all the better. Besides, you know what
Coach always says about never assuming the outcome of a
ball game."

"It ain't over 'til the fat lady sings?"

"No, silly. It ain't over 'til it's over."

"Coach didn't say that. Yogi Berra did."

"Well, Coach says it now."

"All right. All right. So what's the plan?" Ben asked hesitantly.

Matt could tell that his friend wasn't sure about the legiti-
macy of this new scheme. "We take the offence," he offered
quickly. "We're a good team, right?"

Ben nodded in agreement.

"Well, we simply start acting like it. You know how all the
all-star teams in Peterborough are called the Sharks?"

Ben nodded once again.

"Well, I think we should really go with the shark thing.
You know, maybe make up a few shark cheers. We could even
give ourselves shark nicknames. Like Great White for Mike,
because he's so tall and blond. Plus, the great white is really
flexible despite its huge size, just like Mike. I looked over my
project notes today. Steve Hutton could be a speckled cat
shark. We could call him Scat for short."

Ben laughed. Steve's face was covered with freckles, and
he was quick and agile like a cat. Matt had chosen the perfect
name for him. "What did you decide for me?" he asked.

"How about Hammerhead? Just kidding," Matt added,
when he noticed the emerging scowl. "I haven't totally figured everything out yet. But if you really think about it,
Hammerhead isn't all that bad." He flopped himself back into

position on the sofa. "You're the catcher, right? So your head's always getting banged around from balls off the back of the screen or the bat. Plus a hammerhead shark has eyes at both sides of its head. Wouldn't that be a great thing for a catcher to have?"

"Okay, okay," Ben laughed. "Here's the deal."

You can call me Hammerhead, if the rest of us get to call you Megamouth." He had looked over Matt's report earlier. He too had been fascinated by the wide variety of sharks.

Matt quickly agreed. The news about Spike McGarrity had created an extremely obliging atmosphere.

"Maybe we could all get together and practice during the summer holidays. Even if Coach has to work, we could still do it. We're old enough to look after ourselves. And you know that jar of shark teeth that Andy is always talking about? The ones his grandmother collected on the beach in Florida?" The words gushed from Matt's mouth like a tidal wave. He had been thinking about this for more than a week, and he had been waiting all day to share the details of his plan. "Maybe she'd let us have a few. You know, to make those shark tooth necklaces. The guys in the majors are always wearing stuff around their necks. Why couldn't we?"

"I don't think the umps would let us," Ben said, cautiously.

"Well, maybe at practice then," Matt replied.

He was even more excited about this plan than he'd been with the other. Only this one was better. The whole team could get involved this time around. They could even tell Coach Leahy about Shark Attack!

# 14

## School's Out!

A feeling of excitement hovered over East City Bowl the night Matt resumed playing with the team. It was almost as if Coach had substituted a special ingredient when he had lined the diamond that day, magically transforming everything inside the powdery white lines.

The late June air was unusually warm and balmy and school was out for the summer. Best of all, Ben's news had been confirmed. At that very moment, the McGarritys, including Spike, were wending their way over red earthen roads toward Cavendish Beach, Prince Edward Island.

Were there sharks around P.E.I.? Matt wondered. He had seen them in tanks before, but never in the open ocean. It would be an incredible experience to watch their smooth streamlined bodies slicing majestically through the blue-grey surf.

Maybe, he fantasized, the team could recruit a large mako to cruise the beach in search of Spike McGarrity. Matt imagined massive jaws opening wide, swallowing him in one gigantic gulp.

He'd never really want that to happen, he decided, remembering how great Spike had been on the phone. Chuckling at the lunacy of his thoughts, he bent to scoop up the grounder Coach Leahy had sent streaking in his direction. It escaped, under his glove.

"No worries!" Coach shouted, pushing the ball cap off his forehead and wiping a shirtsleeve across his sweaty brow. "You'll be back in the swing of things in no time."

Exactly right, Matt muttered, glaring down at his glove in disbelief. He was going to make sure of that. The East City Sharks didn't need any special tricks or outside interference to defeat the Lions. Spike was expected to miss three games as it was, and depending on their outcome, the Sharks still had a good chance to advance. A great chance, Matt figured, now that he had finally come to his senses. Now that the team had Shark Attack.

Starting today, Matt was going to focus on nothing but ball for the rest of the summer. He was going to direct all his energy toward improving his own skills and helping out the entire team.

The Sharks easily handled the Eagles during Matt's first game back. Their pitching had been a little shaky at times, but their defence had been solid, their hitting strong.

Matt had missed the two previous games — both lopsided victories over the Gators and the Bears, the two weakest teams in the league. As far as ball was concerned, he had timed his suspension perfectly.

Not so with school. Word of Matt's phone call had quickly spread. If only he'd waited a week, he wouldn't have had to face the kids at Queen Elizabeth.

He had felt foolish the first couple of days, but eventually things settled back to normal. All the field trips, class parties, and excitement that accompanied the last week had taken the attention off Matt and had brightened his spirits. Best of all, there had been no homework! That had allowed for extensive contemplation of his latest plan.

Amongst team members, it was unanimous. Shark Attack was deemed, in the words of Mike, Great White, a "whale of an idea."

"You could all come over to my house and work on the cheers," Kate suggested.

"And I'm sure my Grandma would let us have some teeth," Andy Sokoloski offered, proud to be contributing in such a significant manner. "She collects more every year. I'll phone and ask her tonight. What's my nickname?" he asked, curious.

"You guys will all see on Friday," Matt said, "at the game. I should have everything figured out by then." His sand-coloured brows bunched together over the bridge of his nose. The Panthers would not be an easy mark. In the latest league standings they were positioned right below the Sharks, just waiting to creep into second place should they win the weekend matchup.

"Why don't we all go down to Aquamania, the night before the game?" Mike's suggestion wedged its way into Matt's thoughts. "They've got a real live shark in a giant tank and they have a feeding frenzy every Thursday night at seven o'clock." Making a fist with one hand, he forcefully smashed it into his open palm. "That would really pump us up."

"We could eat shark steak before our next game," Steve Hutton said, huge brown eyes round in his small freckled face. "I saw a guy with some once, right behind us at the supermarket checkout. I didn't believe it at first but I looked closer. Sure enough, there it was, in clear black letters, written right on the package: shark steak. It didn't cost that much either."

"Or we could try shark bites," Ryan Bryd added. "You know, those little macaroni thingamajigs my mother buys." He chanted to the beat of the popular old Queen tune. "We will, we will, bite you!"

Quickly, he flipped his ball cap off, shoved the back of the hat forward into the brim and pushed the black peak into position to resemble a shark's fin. Grinning triumphantly, he plunked the finished product on his handsome brown head.

"That looks awesome!" Matt cried. "Look, everybody. Check out Ryan's hat. That could be the rally symbol for the team."

With their hats perched on their heads, shark fins exposed, the team members rocketed to their feet and gathered around Matt in a tight huddle.

"Shark Attack!" they shouted. "Shark Attack!" Their voices rose in unison, confidence growing with each repetition. "SHARK ATTACK!"

# 15

# Shark Infested

Fox," Matt stated firmly. He smiled as he carefully printed the word on the paper in front of him. "Kate can be the fox shark. Her hair is reddish and full and shiny. Looks kinda like a fox's tail, the way she pushes it through the little hole in the back of her ballcap. And none of the other names suit her near as well." He placed his pencil on the table, satisfied.

Tilting back on his wooden chair, Ben nodded in agreement. Originally, he had suggested the cookie-cutter or the grey nurse shark, but Matt was right. Kate would never go for either of those.

"Ben Aoki!" Mr. Tucker's voice sounded gruff and firm.

Ben flinched, then raised his head, alarmed.

"Take it easy on the furniture, please." Matt's dad had quickly adjusted his tone and smiled reassuringly at Ben as he strode through the kitchen into the living room beyond.

Ben's chair thumped back to the floor with a bang. Minou wandered out of the room, her tail lashing from side to side in displeasure.

Matt smiled apologetically. His father had loosened up quite a bit since the phone fiasco and the coach's meeting, that was true. He had been a lot nicer to all of them and he'd been spending more time with Matt, working on his hitting and fielding at the Board of Education field. But his dad would always be his dad, Matt had finally come to realize. His gruff manner didn't mean he hated them or anything. That was just the way he was. Little things mattered to him a lot.

"We can check everything out with Kate tomorrow," Matt calmly added. "When we go over to her place to work on the cheers."

* * *

A handful of players gathered at Kate Crowley's on Wednesday afternoon. Mike, Steve, Chris, Matt, and Ben were there. Steve's little sister had tagged along too, to play with Kate's brother Kyle.

At first they brainstormed, spouting forth every idea that popped into their heads. Then, selecting the best, they worked up chants around those. Matt could hardly wait until the next game to try them out on the opposition.

"What do you think of Kate?" Ben asked, a little later as they left the Crowley's and ambled off in the direction of Pinehill Drive. "I mean really. Do you think she's pretty?" He had tried his best to sound matter of fact, but Matt easily saw through his friend's casual exterior.

"You like her, don't you," Matt teased, an impish smirk spreading slowly over his face.

"She's okay, I guess." Ben hurriedly dropped his eyes. His cheeks flushed. Then suddenly, his entire manner changed. "I'll kill you if you tell anyone," he cried, eyes snapping, voice rising, harsh and threatening.

"I won't. I won't," Matt retorted.

They walked in silence.

Finally Matt spoke up. "No need to worry," he assured his friend. He punched Ben playfully on the arm. "Megamouths can keep a secret, you know."

* * *

Matt presented the complete lineup of nicknames during the warm-up session for Saturday's game against the Panthers. He pulled the crumpled list from his pant's pocket for everyone to see. Even Coach Leahy was there, right at the top of the list.

Coach Leahy — Whitetip (greying black hair)
Ben — Hammerhead (catcher, eyes on both sides of its head)
Mike — Great White (tall, blond)
Steve — Speckled Cat — Scat (freckles, fast and agile)
Chris — Tiger (eats almost anything)
Kate — Fox (red hair, looks like fox's tail)
Ryan — Thresher (long tail to hit and stun opponents)
Andy — Mackerel (likes to fish)
Matt — Megamouth (mouthy, rare breed)
Rob — Horn (plays trumpet in school bands)
Jason — Spiny Dogfish (brushcut)
Tim — Wobbegong (aggressive when under attack)

The new, shark-infested peewee squad was an enormous success. Nicknames were tossed around, dorsal fin caps flashed about, and cheers were chanted continually by those on the bench and eventually by the fans in the stands. The team's enthusiasm was contagious. Several passers-by had even stopped to watch, drawn in by the noise and the keen competition on the playing field.

The Sharks were leading four to three when Matt jogged onto the field for the bottom of the seventh.

"Tight *D*!" reminded Coach Leahy.

"S ... H ... A ... R ... K!" Matt chanted loudly.

"Sharks are gonna win today," added his teammates. Their voices rang with confidence and enthusiasm.

"Three up … three down," responded the parents. "Three up … three down!"

Mrs. Byrd let out a loud whoop and the other parents echoed back.

Matt thumped his glove and leaned forward on the balls of his feet. He would need to concentrate with the top of the order coming to the plate. Any slip-up could cost the Sharks the game.

Chris Kenton walked the first batter.

"No worries," Ben shouted. "You'll get the next one."

Jesse Clancy walked to the plate. He managed a small piece of the first offering but his swing was late. Matt adjusted his defensive position accordingly. The batter worked the count to three and two, then watched in dismay as Chris delivered a heated fastball, catching the outside corner of the plate. "Stee-rike three."

"That's one," Matt shouted to Kate and Andy who were flanking him in centre. "Who wants number two?"

Kate pulled in Cameron O'Connor's long, floating fly ball. She fired it to the cutoff man. Ryan, in turn, hit Steve Hutton covering the bag at second. The runner did not advance.

"Time out!" shouted the umpire, turning to dust off the plate.

Matt chuckled quietly to himself. Chris had once told him how tempted he was just to fire one in when the ump was bending over like that … Focus, he reminded himself. Focus. Here was DesOrmeau, the cleanup hitter for the Panthers. If anyone could give the ball a ride, he was the guy to do it.

"Strike one," boomed the umpire. The batter had let the first pitch go by. DesOrmeau stepped back from the plate, tapped the dirt off his cleats with his bat, then re-entered the box.

Ben chattered nonstop from his crouch behind the plate.

"Atta boy, Tiger baby. No batta here, no batta."

The batter cocked the bat and took a couple of practice rips. He cocked again and took a massive swipe. There was no swish of air this time. Kaboom! The ball exploded off the bat like a bullet — a frozen rope, headed directly for shallow centre.

Matt streaked forward with the blast, eyes glued on the ball, arms pumping. He reached forward with one last massive stretch, then breathed a sigh of relief when he felt the soft smack of ball and leather. Matt carried his momentum forward, charging onto the infield, thrusting his glove high in the air as the entire team converged on the mound.

* * *

After the cheers had subsided and the handshakes and bench cleanup had all taken place, Coach Leahy gathered his team on the grassy green carpet in shallow right field. "I don't know what's gotten into you guys, but after what I've witnessed today, I can see this team is bound and determined to make it to the County Championships."

The Sharks whooped in agreement.

"We're going to meet every morning at the park across from my house for some extra practice," Matt announced. "We know you have to work, but my older brother has already agreed to help us with our batting. And my dad said he could help too, at least one morning a week. He knows a lot about ball."

Coach Leahy stood motionless for a brief moment, eyes gleaming mischievously. Slowly, he rubbed his chin. "Mmmmm, I just might have a few good ideas myself." He paused and looked reproachfully at Matt. "Despite the fact that I'm such an old geezer." Reaching forward he grabbed Matt playfully by the scruff of the neck. "Whitetip, indeed."

"If the fin fits ..." Ryan chuckled.

The entire team hooted with laughter while Matt and Ryan exchanged high-fives.

"Just promise me one thing for now," Coach continued, trying his best to sound serious.

"What's that, Coach?" queried Chris.

"That you'll all be at the next practice." Cracking a smile he added, "Tuesday night. Six o'clock. Shark!"

# 16

## School's In

I'd like to introduce a couple of special people to the team," Coach announced proudly, glancing down at the circle of upturned faces gathered at his feet. He did a double take. Sure enough, every single player was wearing a shark tooth necklace. One large tooth had been securely attached to a thin strip of light brown suede using some type of fine gold-coloured wire.

Puddles of murky water were scattered about the diamond, leftovers from the heavy rain that had fallen during the night. A light wind sent hundreds of water droplets trickling down the ribbed green leaves of the maples. Overhead, rain clouds lingered.

The ground itself was damp and cool, but the Sharks had turned out for the practice in full force, anxious to impress Coach with their new, improved style of play. Four intensive workouts had already produced significant results.

Matt studied the two strangers flanking Coach Leahy. The man had sand-coloured greying hair and was tall, with a ruddy complexion, thick arms, and a friendly face. The woman was darker and much shorter, but she too had a strong athletic build.

"I figured the least I could do was find you guys a little extra help," Coach was saying. "I know the weather isn't the greatest, but a little moisture won't bother you sharks."

Ryan Byrd repositioned his cap with the shark fin exposed and flailed his arms, imitating a shark surfing its way through the waves of the ocean. The others laughed heartily.

"Okay, okay," Coach called a halt to the silliness. He pointed to the man with the muscular arms. "Dave Ruthowsky here is retired now, but he's one of the best softball pitchers living in the Peterborough area. He was one of the best in the world, in fact, back in the '70s."

The visitor's weight shifted uneasily, while Coach continued. "His name was in the *Guinness Book of World Records* for pitching a perfect game at the World Championships in New Zealand in 1976."

Eleven sets of Shark jaws dropped in awe.

"He's going to take the pitchers under his wing, so to speak, for a couple of sessions." Coach stepped forward and stood beside the woman on his opposite side. "And Elaine here, she knows what she's talking about too. She's played senior ball for years. Quite a pitcher in her own right. Won two World Championships in women's softball, one in New Zealand and one in China. But, she's a teacher now and she's good at assessing hitting. She won the MVP at the Canadians, in fact, and her hitting contributed largely to winning that award. Let's just say, if there's anything wrong with your swing, she'll spot it."

Excellent, Matt thought. There was no question about it now. The Lions were definitely going down. "Sharks are gonna rule," he whispered to Ben.

Mentally, Matt assigned each of the newcomers their own shark nickname. Mako for the man, after one of the most powerful and fastest sharks in the sea. "Robust body with pointed snout," the book had also said. Matt smiled to himself. The description seemed to fit.

And the woman Coach had called Elaine? Well, she'd definitely be an angel shark, Matt figured, if she could teach him how to hit speedy Spike McGarrity.

Chris and Mike eagerly followed Dave Ruthowsky to the practice diamond on the opposite side of the park. They worked on perfecting release points, forward strides and hip rotations, and completing follow-throughs. Mr. Ruthowsky also worked on their off-speed pitches, giving them a few pointers for further practice at home.

Both Mike and Chris were a little wild at first, while making the necessary adjustments. After a couple of practices they settled in, hurling faster and more accurately than ever before.

Meanwhile, the others took turns batting under the watchful eye of Elaine Devlin. Matt listened attentively to her every word.

"Keep those eyes fixed right on the ball," Elaine admonished Jason. "Don't spin your head around with your swing. And try and remember, you're playing the ball, not the other team, not the pitcher. You're playing the ball. Watch it come right from the hip."

"No, Andy, try it like this. It's the mid-points of the fingers, the second set of knuckles, that should meet when you grip the bat. It might feel a little uncomfortable at first, if you're not used to doing it, but it will pay off in the long run, giving you maximum speed and power."

"Make sure the bat isn't too heavy," Elaine reminded him. "A lighter bat will increase your swing speed. You should be able to hold your bat perpendicular to your body, parallel to the ground, with just one hand. If you can't, the bat's probably too heavy, especially if the pitcher has good speed," she added.

"Back of the box, Kate," Elaine warned. "If this guy's as fast as Coach Leahy says, and there's no junk on the ball, you'll want to give yourself as much time as possible. Choking up a bit might help. You don't need to worry about a power swing with this guy. You just want to make contact."

"Don't cock the bat so far behind your ears, Tim. Lay it out a little more. Something like this. You can open up that stance a little too. You can spot that ball a little easier."

With Elaine's guidance, the Sharks' hitting dramatically improved. Combined with the excellent pitching of Mike and Chris, the team rapidly accumulated points. By the time Spike McGarrity returned to the rubber, Shark Attack had taken an enormous toll.

# 17

# Battle of the Best

Matt, Ben, and Kate tentatively eyed the steaming contents of the platter Marg Tucker placed in the centre of the kitchen table. Blue Willow, she had called the plate, and she had tucked little bits of leafy green parsley all around the edge.

"Your mom's a good sport," Kate said. "My mom thinks the whole team's gone crazy. Thanks for letting me come by. It really is a great idea," she continued, crinkling up her short pert nose, "to actually become part shark for the game. Only problem is, I don't know if I'll be able to eat this stuff. It smells a little too fishy for me."

"You taste it first," Ben suggested, looking squarely at Matt. "This is all part of your plan, remember?"

"Don't be such wimps," Matt retorted, moving a small piece of the fish onto the plate in front of him. "We all promised. Everyone else is having shark steak for lunch today."

Today was the day, the day of the big game, the biggest game of the year. There it stood in large, boldface type on the front page of the sports section of *The Peterborough Examiner*. Matt had clipped it for his scrapbook, just the night before.

**BATTLE OF THE BEST**
Peterborough's own peewee fastball team,
the East City Sharks, host season rival, the

Lakefield Lions, in a sudden death matchup tomorrow afternoon at East City Bowl. These two teams tied for first place after regular season action, necessitating the post-season showdown. Tomorrow's winner will advance to the Tri-County Championships.

Although both squads have had impressive seasons, the Lions, led by pitching ace Spike McGarrity, are heavily favoured. This team has remained undefeated whenever young McGarrity has been on the mound.

"But don't count the Sharks out," says Coach Leahy, the man at the helm of the Sharks' coaching staff. "These kids have really improved since last meeting the Lions. And they're hungry!" He urges local fans to come out at 1:00 p.m. to not only support the local team, but to catch some of the finest minor league fastball in Ontario.

"How's the shark?" Matt's dad had wandered into the kitchen, video camera clasped firmly in his hand. Hoisting it to eye level, he directed it at Matt. "Let me get a shot of the pre-game festivities."

The three ball players repositioned their caps shark style and clowned for the camera.

Matt's mom broke a small piece of the shark steak off his piece and placed it in her mouth. She chewed slowly, deliberately. "Mmmm," she murmured, "not bad at all, considering the fact that I had no idea how to cook this stuff. It's a good thing I ran into Mrs. Stephenson at the grocery store. 'Just wrap it in foil and toss it on the barbeque,' she said."

Matt poked at the shark with the tines of his fork. A small white chunk fell off, then separated into layers. Just like tuna, he thought, pushing a small piece into his mouth. Mom was right, he decided. It was really pretty good. If she was right about it being brain food and high in protein, the Lions would be, well … they'd be dead meat.

* * *

Batting practice was already underway when the three friends arrived at the diamond. Several of the Lions were there too, loosening up, their gold and black uniforms providing a colourful contrast to the leafy green backdrop of the maples.

Excitement bubbled inside Matt. This was it! Everything they'd been working for all summer long was on the line today. His stomach knotted with nervousness.

Both teams took their practice infield as more and more fans drifted into the park. Despite the size of the crowd, the mood was quiet, subdued. Matt could feel the tension mounting.

Coach Leahy gathered the Sharks about him under the scoreboard in right field for a last-minute pep talk. "This is a big game," he stated calmly. "We all know that." He studied the anxious faces of the players and smiled warmly. "Relax out there today, okay? Just give it your best shot. That's all I expect. Win or lose, we've had a great season." He slapped a couple of players on the back. "Go have some fun! Okay?"

Matt felt the knot in the pit of his stomach loosen as the team leapt to its feet, hats pushed into the now familiar rally pose.

"Shark Attack!" they shouted. "Shark Attack!"

Jogging easily, glove and warm-up ball tucked securely under his arm, Matt led the procession onto the playing field. "S … H … A … R … K.!" he cried.

"Sharks are gonna win today!" his teammates responded.

"Squish the fish!" heckled a young Lions fan.

The Lakefield side of the diamond erupted in laughter.

Lions, Lions,
Hear us roar.
Let's beat those Sharks.
Let's score, score, score.

"Three up! Three down!" retorted the Shark supporters. "Three up! Three down!"

"We're the Sharks," shouted Matt from centre.

"Hungry, hungry Sharks!"

Mike, Great White, finally took the mound for the home team. He readjusted his cap and fired a few warm-up pitches to Ben.

Short, but speedy, Brett West led off for the Lions.

Matt punched his glove, chattered encouragingly to Mike, then leaned forward on the balls of his feet in anticipation.

"Strike!" the umpire boomed, as the first pitch blazed by, armpit high, catching the outside corner.

Brett squared around on the next pitch, sending a soft dribbler rolling down the third base line. Rob Tivy darted forward like a beagle, eyes tracking the ball, nose glued to the ground. In one fluid motion, he had scooped and fired to Steve Hutton covering the bag at first.

"Thatta way, guys," Coach yelled. "Show 'em your stuff."

The Sharks gunned the white ball around the horn, then returned it to Mike on the mound. The tall right-hander leaned back confidently and delivered. He mowed the next two batters down in order.

Lately, Matt had been batting in leadoff position for the Sharks. He checked the clothespin contraption the coach had rigged together and hooked to the Sharks' corner of the backstop. It let the players easily see the order of batters and allowed for quick changes to the lineup. Sure enough, there was Matt — the first peg attached to the long wooden dowel.

Only instead of the usual, Matt T., the clothespin now read Megamouth. Matt smiled.

He took a few practice swings and stepped anxiously to the plate. Breathing deeply, he scratched out a shallow footing in the dirt and stared into his opponent's eyes. He'd been hitting well lately, but could he do the same against Spike? This would be the test of that, he decided, bracing himself for the pitch.

Spike smoked the first one down the centre of the plate and grinned complacently.

"Don't be afraid to let one go by," Elaine had said. "Get the feel of it."

The next two pitches were balls. Two and one, gesticulated the tall masked man behind the plate.

Matt took a smooth swipe at the fourth pitch, solidly fouling it down the third base line. Spike, surprised Matt had gotten such good wood on the ball, bore down hard.

"You've got his number," Coach shouted as Matt returned to the bench a few seconds later. "You'll straighten it out next time."

"Drat!" Matt mumbled to himself, placing his bat in the rack behind the screen. He'd been so close he had almost tasted it.

"You've got his number?" Ben joked. "I think it's the other way around — remember, call display."

Matt punched Ben playfully on the arm. "We were all going to forget about that. Wasn't that what coach said?"

Who would be the first to get a hit off Spike McGarrity? It didn't really matter, Matt told himself, as long as someone did. As long as the Sharks beat the Lions.

In the top of the second, Great White had trouble with his control, but the tight defence of his teammates kept the Shark shutout intact.

Spike cut the Sharks down in order once again.

"We're the Lions!" Rob Flamminio shouted, racing off the field, arms and legs pumping wildly.

"Mighty, mighty Lions!" the others chanted back, smacking their mitts.

"We're the Sharks!" Matt replied cockily, charging onto the diamond.

"Hungry, hungry Sharks!" his teammates cried.

"Top of the order," Coach reminded the squad. "Let's see if we can hold 'em."

Brett popped up. Brad singled. Robbie walked. Then Spike McGarrity strode purposefully to the plate. The tall capable pitcher took a few massive swipes of the air with his bat, wibble-wobbled it confidently about his shoulders, then cocked it and waited for the pitch.

Mike scowled. The umpire crouched. The crowd hushed expectantly.

A trail of noisy preschoolers scurried by the back of the screen. The Laporte's black-and-white terrier barked at a squirrel as it scampered up the trunk of a nearby tree. But all eyes were focused on Spike at the plate as the pitch zoomed in ...

CRACK! Shark fans watched in horror as the ball rocketed down the third base line. Spike tore toward first while Brad rounded the bag at third and raced for home. Katie gunned a beautiful peg to the plate, but it was too late.

After the dust had settled, the scoreboard read Lions one, Sharks zero. And runners on second and third, Matt thought. Things were looking grim for the Sharks.

Coach Leahy called time. He walked toward the pitcher's circle and motioned for Mike to replace Andy in right field. He waved Chris in from the warm-up screen and onto the rubber. Two strikeouts later, they were out of the inning.

Heads down, shoulders hunched, the Sharks jogged slowly off the field. Matt glanced over his shoulder at the scoreboard and grimaced. One run was a big lead with Spike McGarrity on the mound.

The Sharks continued to sparkle defensively, while Spike carried the game for the opposition. Jason and Rob fielded two bunts perfectly, Ben pegged out a runner trying to steal second, and Ryan, Steve, and Jason executed a flawless double-play. Matt himself pulled in Spike's sixth inning blast with a sensational diving snatch in shallow centre.

Offensively, however, the Sharks struggled. By the bottom of the seventh inning, most of the fans, as well as the players, felt that the final outcome had been determined. Spike, it seemed, was just too good, too fast, too perfect.

Not so with Matt. "Remember what Coach always tells us," he reminded the team as he moved toward the on-deck circle.

"Yah, yah, we know ... " Ben drawled from the bench. "It ain't over 'til it's over."

"Come on, you guys. Let's not give up," Matt pleaded. "We've worked too hard. We can still do it." He adjusted his cap rally style and began to chant.

"Shark Attack! Shark Attack!"

The others joined in halfheartedly. "You just can't beat the red, white, and black."

There were already two outs, when, moments later, the energetic captain approached the plate. "Time!" cried Coach. He beckoned to the centre fielder for a conference at third. "Think you can lay down a bunt?"

Matt looked apprehensive.

"The catcher's having a hard time hanging onto the ball. If we can just get someone on base, maybe we can somehow squeeze that run across." Coach slapped Matt on the back.

"Just square around good and early and lay it down. You can do it," he added encouragingly.

Matt stepped up to the plate and shuffled himself into position between the chalky white lines of the batter's box. He gripped the bat nervously between his moist warm hands, his mind racing. Ben and Steve had both tried bunting earlier, but they had failed. What made Coach think he could do it?

Matt gulped, took a few practice rips to throw the Lions off guard, then squared around with the pitch. Like a cobra striking, he stabbed.

"Too anxious," he muttered. "Too anxious." He'd been working on his bunt with his brother all week, he reminded himself. Just pretend it's Kevin out there.

This time his execution was much cleaner.

"Foul ball," bellowed the umpire.

Matt backed out of the box and glanced down at Coach Leahy. Flamminio had retreated to third and was chattering nonstop from his position adjacent to the bag. Coach was thoughtfully rubbing his chin, sizing up the situation.

Finally, Coach drew an $X$ across his chest, touched his cap, his ear, and shoved his hands deep in his pockets. Matt stared at the coach in disbelief. He repeated the signal.

Did Coach Leahy know what he was doing? Matt returned hesitantly to the box. Nobody bunted on their third strike. Why, if the ball went foul he'd be out.

Suddenly, he repositioned himself, pulled his lower lip between his teeth and frowned determinedly. Spike eyed him back with a fierce scowl.

Matt cocked his bat one last time and as Spike reached the top of his Ferris wheel motion, Matt pivoted. Maybe he was a little early, he feared; it was the quickest he had ever squared. But for some reason, he felt in control. The timing was good.

He let the bat absorb the ball while he directed it ever so gently in the direction of third base.

Flamminio, standing flat-footed by the bag, stumbled forward, scrambling frantically. The crowd rose to its feet in unison as Matt streaked down the lime-lined alleyway toward first base.

# 18

## Hungry, Hungry Sharks

Shark Attack!
Shark Attack!
You just can't beat,
The red, white, and black!

The Shark bench had sprung to life.

Mr. Crowley stood in the coach's box at first, left arm circling madly, right arm pointing at second as the throw sailed high over the first-baseman's head. The right fielder had forgotten to cover the bag on the throw. He hustled after the ball, then hurled it to third.

Rob Flamminio was out of position. He was down the line glaring at Spike who had reprimanded him for his wild throw. The ball darted past both players and careened off the screen.

Matt had already rounded second and was nearing third. "Keep going!" Coach screamed, waving him on. "Take home!"

Spike lunged after the ball while Matt caught the inside corner of the bag with his left foot and streaked, heart pounding, for home.

A few seconds later, Matt saw the Lion's catcher position himself at the plate and reach for the ball. He saw his own legs shoot out from underneath him. But after that, it was all a blur: a tangle of arms, legs, glove, ball, and dust.

The fans and players from both teams were still on their feet, voices hushed, waiting with excitement and anticipation for the call of the hovering umpire.

Matt lay on the ground for a few seconds, dazed. Finally, he realized, more from the reaction of the fans than anything else, that he was out. He was out. The game was over. The Sharks had lost. He could feel the tears filling his eyes as he picked himself up out of the dirt.

The Lions poured onto the infield and pounced on Spike. Matt blinked hard, but one tear managed to leak out, trickling its way down the flushed and dusty cheek. If only he'd ran a little faster. Maybe if he'd started his slide a little earlier. If only ...

Suddenly, Coach Leahy was there beside him, followed by Ben and the rest of the team. They were happily slapping him on the back. "Whatta bunt! Whatta slide!"

The parents and fans of the Sharks streamed onto the diamond. Matt watched in awe from the centre of the boisterous, congratulating group.

"That's the best game I've seen in years," Mr. Earle was declaring. "You kids can really play ball."

"That's what I call entertainment!" Mrs. Freeburn beamed proudly at her son. "I wouldn't have missed that game for the world." She directed her gaze at Mrs. Tucker. "It's amazing how they've all improved so much this year."

The Bryds were there too, Mrs. Byrd with camera in hand, snapping proudly, stealing candid shots for the team's scrapbook.

Matt heard his own father congratulate the coaches of the Sharks. He pumped both their hands excitedly. "You guys did a super job. I really think you had to go for it there, when you had the chance. I would have tried the same thing." He strode toward Matt and put one arm about his son's shoulders. "What a terrific bunt! And that was some catch you made in the top of the sixth. You all did a great job out there today!"

Matt yanked off his helmet and grinned radiantly. The sickening pangs of disappointment and defeat had totally disappeared. It didn't make sense. They'd lost the game, but for some reason he was starting to feel pretty good about himself.

"Three cheers for the Lions!" Matt shouted.

"Hip, hip, hoo-ray!" his teammates answered.

"Three cheers for the Sharks!" Matt's voice rang with enthusiasm.

The fans and players joined in heartily in response.

As the two teams shook hands for one last time, Matt couldn't help but notice — the Lions' smiles didn't seem quite as broad; their parents not nearly so proud and excited.

"Mr. Tucker." Coach Leahy pulled Matt's dad aside as Mary Byrd began to gather the players for a team photo.

Matt trotted off with the others, then suddenly, he pivoted. He wanted to make sure his dad got this on video.

Coach Leahy was deep in conversation with Mr. Tucker when Matt approached the two men from behind. "I don't want Matt to know yet," Coach was saying, "but he'll be named the team's Most Improved Player at the banquet this year."

"Great!" Mr. Tucker responded. "Matt will really be pleased."

Matt had stopped short when he had heard his name. His smile broadened as he listened attentively.

"I want all the parents to be aware," Coach continued. "You know, so you can bring your camera, that type of thing. Matt got off to a slow start, but he sure turned himself around mid-season."

John Tucker rubbed his chin and nodded thoughtfully.

Matt quickly turned and joined the others. He didn't want his father or his coach to know he had overheard the entire conversation. It was funny how things had worked out. He'd forgotten all about a trophy.

"Come on, Coach," cried Mrs. Byrd. "We need you for the pictures. Mr. Crowley, too."

Mr. Tucker hadn't needed Matt's reminder after all. He had followed the others and was moving into position to capture the final moment of the season on film.

* * *

After the cameras had been put away, Coach spoke quietly to a few more of the parents. Then he made his way over to the Sharks who still lingered around the backstop verbally reliving the action. "Anybody hungry?" he called.

The response was unanimous.

"How about heading over to the Dairy Dream for a final post-game celebration? My treat," he added.

"All right!" shouted Ben.

"We're the Sharks," Matt chanted happily.

"Hungry, hungry, Sharks!" the others added, laughing.

Coach Leahy pretended to glance in his wallet in horror.

"Look out, Dairy Dream," Matt called as he turned his hat into the East City Sharks rally position.

"Shark Attack!" the team shouted in unison. "SHARK ATTACK!"

## Gymnastics

☐ *The Perfect Gymnast* by Michele Martin Bossley #9
Abby's new friend has all the confidence she lacks, but she also has a serious problem that nobody but Abby seems to know about.

## Ice hockey

☐ *Two Minutes for Roughing* by Joseph Romain #2
As a new player on a tough Toronto hockey team, Les must fight to fit in.

☐ *Hockey Night in Transcona* by John Danakas #7
Cody Powell gets promoted to the Transcona Sharks' first line, bumping out the coach's son who's not happy with the change.

☐ *Face Off* by Chris Forsyth #13
A talented hockey player finds himself competing with his best friend for a spot on a select team.

☐ *Hat Trick* by Jacqueline Guest #20
The only girl on an all-boys' hockey team works to earn the captain's respect and her mother's approval.

☐ *Hockey Heroes* by John Danakas #22
A left-winger on the thirteen-year-old Transcona Sharks adjusts to a new best friend and his mom's boyfriend.

☐ *Hockey Heatwave* by Chris Forsyth #27
In this sequel to *Face Off*, Zack and Mitch encounter some trouble when it looks like only one of them will make the select team at hockey camp.

## Riding

☐ *A Way With Horses* by Peter McPhee #11
A young Alberta rider invited to study show jumping at a posh local riding school uncovers a secret.

☐ *Riding Scared* by Marion Crook #15
A reluctant new rider struggles to overcome her fear of horses.

☐ *Katie's Midnight Ride* by C.A. Forsyth #16
An ambitious barrel racer finds herself without a horse weeks before her biggest rodeo.

☐ *Glory Ride* by Tamara L. Williams #21
Chloe Anderson fights memories of a tragic fall for a place on the Ontario Young Riders' Team.

☐ *Cutting it Close* by Marion Crook #24
In this novel about barrel racing, a talented young rider finds her horse is in trouble just as she is about to compete in an important event.

## Roller hockey

☐ *Roller Hockey Blues* by Steven Barwin and Gabriel David Tick #17
Mason Ashbury faces a summer of boredom until he makes the roller-hockey team.

## Sailing

☐ *Sink or Swim* by William Pasnak #5
Dario can barely manage the dog paddle but thanks to his mother he's spending the summer at a water sports camp.

## Soccer

☐ *Lizzie's Soccer Showdown* by John Danakas #3
When Lizzie asks why the boys and girls can't play together, she finds herself the new captain of the soccer team.

## Swimming

☐ *Breathing Not Required* by Michele Martin Bossley #4
An eager synchronized swimmer works hard to be chosen for a solo and almost loses her best friend in the process.

☐ *Water Fight!* by Michele Martin Bossley #14
Josie's perfect sister is driving her crazy but when she takes up swimming — Josie's sport — it's too much to take.